Frankenstein's Bride: A Mystery

Circle of Roses, Volume 1

Martha Wickham

Published by Martha Wickham, 2020.

FRANKENSTEIN'S BRIDE: A MYSTERY

First edition. October 25, 2020.

ISBN: 979-8231124220

Written by Martha Wickham.

Table of Contents

Frankenstein's Bride: A Mystery

The murky water of the swamp clung to Frankenstein's heavy boots, each step a reluctant, wet release. The air hung thick and humid, a breeding ground for unseen insects that buzzed incessantly around his crudely stitched face. He moved with a singular, brutal purpose, the image of the watching man etched into his primitive memory. The man's eyes, wide with a terror that mirrored the creature's own internal chaos, had been the spark that ignited this latest surge of rage.

He reached the edge of the water, his immense form casting a distorted shadow on the damp earth. The man stood frozen, a silhouette against the dimming twilight, his hand instinctively reaching toward his throat as if already feeling the crushing grip. A woman beside him gasped, a small, sharp sound that only fueled Frankenstein's fury. It was the sound of fear, the sound he had come to associate with his very existence.

With a guttural roar that tore through the stillness, Frankenstein lunged. The distance between them vanished in an instant. His large, calloused hands, capable of such delicate construction yet now instruments of destruction, clamped around the man's neck. The man thrashed, his eyes bulging, his breath escaping in strangled gasps. The woman screamed, a high-pitched, sustained sound that echoed through the trees, but Frankenstein remained focused on his victim, the raw power in his grip unrelenting. In a matter of moments, the struggling ceased, and the man slumped lifelessly to the ground.

Frankenstein stood over his fallen prey, his chest heaving, a strange mix of satisfaction and emptiness churning within him. He had silenced the fear, but it did not quell the turmoil in his soul. The woman had fled, her screams fading into the distance. He turned his gaze towards the city, a distant cluster of lights that seemed to mock his isolation. A deadly resolve hardened within him. He would make them understand his pain, the torment of his unnatural existence. He would make them fear him as he feared himself.

His rampage began slowly, almost hesitantly at first. He moved through the outskirts of the city like a phantom, his immense size surprisingly allowing for a degree of stealth. He overturned carts, the clatter and splintering wood a small prelude to the terror to come. He frightened lone travelers, their panicked cries a fleeting echo of his own constant anguish. But it was not enough. The whispers of fear were too quiet, too easily swallowed by the vastness of the city. He needed to make a statement, a grand, terrifying declaration of his unwanted existence.

He found himself drawn to a large stone structure, its imposing facade radiating an air of permanence and indifference. It was a place of authority, a place where perhaps the very people who had condemned him might reside. He crept towards it, his heavy footsteps muffled by the soft earth. He knew he had been seen; fleeting glimpses of startled faces at windows confirmed it. But he no longer cared about stealth. He wanted them to see him, to witness the horror they had wrought.

He pushed open the heavy oak doors, the groan of the ancient hinges echoing through the silent interior. The air inside was cool and smelled of dust and old paper. He moved through the dimly lit corridors, his massive frame dwarfing the ornate surroundings. He left a trail of destruction in his wake – overturned furniture, shattered glass, ripped tapestries – each act a small release of his pent-up fury.

Meanwhile, the groundskeeper, an elderly man with a stooped posture and trembling hands, had witnessed Frankenstein's approach from his small cottage near the entrance. He had seen the hulking figure disappear into the stone building and knew instinctively that something terrible was about to unfold. Fear lent him a surprising burst of speed as he fled toward the main part of the city, hoping to raise the alarm. In his haste, he knocked over a lantern he had left burning near a stack of discarded wood. The flickering flame caught quickly, licking at the dry timber. A small wooden chair nearby was the first to succumb, the flames greedily consuming its aged frame.

The fire spread rapidly, the dry wood acting as perfect tinder. Smoke began to billow from the windows of the stone structure, a dark plume against the night sky. The alarm had been raised. A group of villagers, their faces grim and determined, arrived armed with torches and makeshift weapons. They numbered thirty-five, a significant force, and their collective anger and fear gave them a courage they might not have possessed individually. They had heard tales of the creature, whispers of death and destruction, and they were resolved to stop him. The news of the five lives already taken fueled their resolve.

Frankenstein, alerted by the growing commotion outside and the acrid smell of smoke, retreated deeper into the building. He was a creature of instinct as much as rage, and the heat and the growing light were instinctively threatening. He headed toward the back of the structure, hoping to find another exit. But the fire was spreading quickly, engulfing the front door in a roaring inferno, effectively cutting off the villagers' most direct route.

Just then, a figure emerged from the growing crowd, his silhouette familiar and yet somehow smaller, more fragile than Frankenstein remembered. It was Dr. Victor Frankenstein, his creator, his tormentor. His face was pale in the flickering torchlight, his eyes wide with a mixture of horror and a desperate kind of scientific curiosity.

"Why have you done this?" shouted a man from the crowd, his voice thick with anger and grief.

Dr. Frankenstein flinched, his gaze fixed on the burning building. "It was... an experiment," he replied nervously, the words barely audible above the crackling flames and the murmuring of the villagers.

"Just tell us what to do," another voice called out from the crowd, a plea for guidance in the face of this terrifying reality.

"Find him, and lock him away," suggested someone, a desperate attempt to contain the uncontainable.

"That's all we can do," a man said grimly. "Is there another way in?" he asked Dr. Frankenstein, his eyes fixed on the inferno.

"Through the back," the mad scientist replied, his voice barely a whisper.

The villagers surged towards the back of the building, their torches casting long, dancing shadows. But as they rounded the corner, the thick smoke and intense heat warned them away. Even if it looked like there might be a way in, the danger was palpable. Through a window three stories up, they could see a large, shadowy figure.

"Fire bad," a deep, guttural voice rumbled, the words strangely childlike yet filled with a primal fear. And then the figure was gone, disappearing from the window. A moment later, a downstairs window shattered, and Frankenstein burst out, heading towards the dark, beckoning expanse of the deep woods.

The villagers, their initial rage tempered by the sight of the fire and the creature's escape, quickly filled their buckets with water, forming a human chain to douse the flames before they could spread to the nearby woods. It was a desperate effort, the fire a terrifying symbol of the chaos Frankenstein had unleashed.

When the flames were finally under control, a large group of men and women ventured into the woods, their torches casting flickering circles of light in the darkness. They searched for hours, their calls echoing through the trees, but Frankenstein was gone.

Back in the town, fear lingered like a heavy fog. Many kept their doors locked and their eyes open, scanning the shadows for any sign of the monster. There was much talk, hushed whispers in the streets and anxious conversations in homes. Some speculated that he might have collapsed from exhaustion or injury, perhaps even met a second, more permanent death in the wilderness.

His bride, Terra Green, still lived, though her existence was a strange twilight between life and death. A few cautious townsfolk kept a watchful eye on her isolated dwelling, a silent reminder of Dr. Frankenstein's hubris and the terror it had spawned. That was all that remained, the lingering fear and the unnatural existence of the Bride, a testament to the experiment that had gone so horribly wrong.

Dr. Frankenstein himself was later warned by the local police, a stern admonishment that seemed woefully inadequate in the face of the destruction and death his creation had caused. He remained a pariah, haunted by the consequences of his ambition, forever linked to the monster that now roamed free.

The Bride of Frankenstein, or Terra Green as she had once been known, sat upon her ornate, high-backed chair, a relic from a time when she had breathed and lived a more conventional life. Now, the velvet felt cold beneath her unnaturally still form. She listened to the wireless radio crackle with news, her black lips, a stark contrast to her pale complexion, curved downwards in a perpetual frown.

"Another body has been found in the wheat field," the announcer's voice droned, each word a leaden weight in the silent room. "It looks like another victim of Dr. Frankenstein's experiment." The news confirmed her deepest fears. Her fiancé, the creature cobbled together from grave robbings and sparked to a gruesome imitation of life, would not be returning to her anytime soon. Not if he was leaving a trail of bodies in his wake.

A strange, morbid understanding bound them. They were both undead, both unnatural, both engaged in a bizarre pact forged in the cold fires of reanimation. And they both shared a visceral, primal hatred of fire, the element that threatened their fragile, borrowed existence. Yet, there was a chasm growing between them, a dark gulf carved by his senseless violence against the living, the very beings she had once been.

She sat and drifted into a melancholic reverie, her thoughts turning to the fleeting joys of her short, mortal life. She had loved before, known the warmth of human connection. But there was one love that burned brighter in her decaying heart, a memory that time and undeath could not extinguish. Nathaniel Johnston, a banker from Chicago, had stolen her heart during the summer of 1926. He had been everything she had ever desired – tall, with eyes as dark and deep as a moonless night, and a handsome smile that could melt away her deepest anxieties.

They had dated, their connection deepening with each shared glance and whispered secret. They had been deeply in love, making plans for a future that now seemed like a distant, impossible dream. They weren't married, but their commitment was as strong as any vow. Then, the cruel hand of fate had intervened. She had fallen ill with pneumonia, her lungs filling with fluid, her life extinguished at the tender age of thirty.

In the strange, minimal space after death, she had found herself inexplicably aware of Nathaniel's continued existence. She had watched over him, a silent, spectral guardian, her love an invisible shield. But now, a cold fury began to simmer within her, directed squarely at Frankenstein. How could he, the being she was meant to spend eternity with, commit such atrocities? How could he stain the memory of her past life, the life she had shared with Nathaniel?

Without conscious thought, she rose, her unnatural strength surging. She picked up a heavy oak table beside her, a piece of furniture that would have required the combined effort of several living men to lift. With a guttural growl of rage, she hurled it across the room. It crashed against the stone wall, shattering into splinters and sending dust motes dancing in the dim light.

"He will not do this," she hissed, her voice a low, rasping sound that echoed the decay within her. "I will not marry him. I never want to see him again."

Her decision made, a strange sense of calm descended upon her. She turned and entered her bedroom, the image of Nathaniel Johnston filling her thoughts. It was time. Time to see him again, even if only for a fleeting glimpse. A longing so intense it felt like a physical ache consumed her.

She lay down on her large, four-poster bed, the white lace of her long dress a stark contrast to the pallor of her skin and the darkness of her hair. Her eyes fluttered closed, and she drifted into a deep, dark, deathly sleep, a state that was now as familiar as waking.

When she awoke, the moon hung high in the inky sky, casting long, eerie shadows across the landscape. She rose from her bed, her movements silent and fluid, and made her way out of her isolated dwelling. She moved like a ghost through the night, her white dress blending with the pale moonlight.

She snuck by the white picket fence surrounding Nathaniel's former home, her heart pounding with a mixture of anticipation and trepidation. She inched slowly towards the front door, peering through the window. She didn't see Nathaniel's car, a familiar Ford Model T, parked in the driveway, so she assumed he wasn't home.

A wave of disappointment washed over her, but she pressed on. Heading towards his old bedroom window on the side of the house, she rounded the corner and suddenly froze. Standing in the yard was a woman, her figure bathed in the moonlight. As Terra turned, a strange transformation occurred. Her spectral form solidified, her white dress seeming to coalesce into a more conventional garment, and a black hat appeared upon her head. She looked like a curious visitor, out for a late-night stroll.

"Is there something you want?" the woman asked, her voice carrying a note of polite inquiry.

"I'm an old girlfriend of Nathan Johnston," Terra replied, her voice a little breathless. "Is he here?"

The woman's expression softened. "No," she said gently. "This *was* his house. We live here now. He died a year ago."

Bride's mouth dropped open in shock. The words hit her like a physical blow, and a coldness spread through her unnatural heart. "What happened?" she asked, her voice barely a whisper, filled with a pain that transcended even her undead existence.

"Car accident," Elisabeth replied, her eyes filled with a genuine sorrow. "He was driving at night where there were no streetlights. It was so sudden. We loved this house, so after everything, we bought it. I'm Elisabeth," she added, holding out her hand in a gesture of comfort.

"I'm Terra," she replied, shaking Elisabeth's hand, her own trembling slightly despite her lack of a beating heart. The bad news had shaken her to her core.

Elisabeth's gaze lingered on Terra's attire – the long, white, somewhat ethereal dress. It wasn't very becoming for a lady making a late-night call. Her stark black hair and equally dark lips also struck Elisabeth as unusual. She wondered why. "I'm so sorry for the bad news," she repeated softly.

"Is he buried here in Chicago?" Terra asked, her voice filled with a desperate urgency. "I need to visit. He meant so much to me."

"Yes, right here in the town cemetery square," Elisabeth nodded, offering a small, sad smile.

"Thank you," Bride said in a low, graceful voice, a remnant of her former life. Elisabeth simply nodded in return. Night was deepening as Terra turned and walked towards the cemetery, the weight of her grief a heavy shroud around her. Stars began to sparkle in the vast expanse of the sky as she reached her destination, the silent rows of headstones stretching out before her like an army of the forgotten.

It did not take long to find the grave. The simple stone marker bore his name: Nathaniel Johnston, 1896-1926. Tears, cold and unnatural, welled in her eyes. She hugged the cold stone, pressing her lips against the etched letters of his name, a silent communion with the man she had loved and lost. Then, with a newfound resolve, she turned and quickly made her way back home, a singular purpose forming in her mind. She needed a large shovel.

Digging in the cool night air did not scare her. Death was no longer a mystery, and the graveyard felt strangely familiar. An owl hooted nearby, its mournful call a fitting soundtrack to her grim task. Finally, the shovel struck something solid. Knock, knock, she hit the wooden coffin. With renewed effort, she cleared the remaining earth and pried open the lid.

She got out of the grave and sat against the tombstone once again, the weight of the unearthed coffin a dark presence beside her. She hugged the cold stone, a strange sense of peace settling over her amidst the macabre scene. "We will be together soon," she whispered into the silent night.

A cold breeze rustled through the trees, sending a shiver down her unnatural spine. She jumped back into the grave and quickly opened the coffin. The sight that greeted her was far more gruesome than she had anticipated. He had been dead for a while, the natural processes of decomposition having taken their toll. But more disturbingly, his body was dismembered, limbs severed, and his head detached. Crude stitches held him back together, but some of the thick black thread had come undone, revealing the unnatural joins. His skin had taken on a light purple hue, the color of stagnant water under a bruised sky.

Despite the horrifying state of his remains, love, or what remained of it in her undead heart, surged through her. She lifted his cold, dismembered head and pressed a kiss to his decaying lips.

With a strength born of desperation, she carefully pieced his body back together as best she could within the confines of the coffin. Then, with a monumental effort, she pushed the heavy wooden box out of the grave and began to drag it towards her isolated abode, the sound of scraping wood and shifting earth the only witnesses to her bizarre pilgrimage.

Back in her dwelling, she laid Nathaniel's remains on the floor beside the crackling fire. The warmth did little to dispel the chill that clung to his decaying flesh. Methodically, she began the gruesome task of reassembling him. With thick black thread and a large needle, she painstakingly sewed the loose body parts back together, her movements precise despite the macabre nature of the work.

Once the crude repairs were complete, she carefully carried his reassembled form down to the dusty, forgotten depths of what used to be Dr. Frankenstein's laboratory before he had met his end at the hands of his own creation. The air in the lab was thick with the smell of decay and forgotten chemicals. Cobwebs draped across the antiquated equipment, and shadows danced in the faint moonlight filtering through a grimy window.

She laid Nathaniel on the large, metal-topped table that had once been the catalyst for Frankenstein's unnatural awakening. The remnants of wires and electrodes still lay scattered across the surface. With trembling hands, she connected similar wires to Nathaniel's reanimated form, mimicking the process that had brought her back from the dead.

She paused, her gaze fixed on his still, purple form. A strange mix of hope and fear churned within her. She wanted to be with him, to rekindle the love they had shared in life, even in this grotesque imitation of it.

The old house moaned around her, the settling timbers and drafts creating eerie sounds in the stillness. A bright, full moon shone through the small, grimy window, casting an ethereal glow on the scene. Taking a deep, unnatural breath, she pulled a large, rusty switch on a nearby machine. Nothing happened. She tried again. Still Silence. Frustration gnawed at her. She jiggled the switch, then slammed her hand against the side of the machine. With a protesting groan of old gears, a dim, flickering light sputtered to life above the table. It was a galvanism lamp, its glass casing cracked and dusty. As it flickered, a shower of tiny glass shards rained down, scattering on the cold stone floor.

She tried the main power switch again. This time, with a loud crackle and a surge of energy, the machine whirred to life. Blue sparks danced between the wires connected to Nathaniel. His body on the table jerked violently. No life. Just a grotesque puppet show powered by unnatural forces.

Despair threatened to engulf her, but she fought it back. She turned off the machine, waited a moment, and then flipped the switch back on. More blue sparks, more violent jerking. This time, his leg twitched. A small, involuntary movement, but a movement nonetheless. Hope flickered within her like the dying embers of a forgotten fire.

She repeated the process, turning the machine off and on, each surge of electricity a desperate plea to the dormant life within him. Finally, with a loud crack and a shower of bright blue sparks, Nathaniel's eyes snapped open. They were a startling, unnatural green, glowing faintly in the dim light of the lab. He sat bolt upright on the table, his stitched limbs moving stiffly.

"Terra?" he croaked, his voice a raspy whisper, like the rustling of dry leaves. Then he groaned, a sound of confusion and pain.

With a cry of joy, Terra rushed to him, embracing his cold, stitched form. "Yes, Nathan! It's me. I needed to see you. I still love you. I just found out you were dead. Now we will be together forever."

His green eyes, still unfocused, slowly began to register her presence. A flicker of recognition, a spark of something that might have once been love, ignited within them. "I would really like that," he said, his voice gaining a little strength. "More than that cold, solitary grave! You and I will be together here." He cleared his dead throat, a rattling sound that sent a shiver down Terra's spine. "Let's do it."

A thought, a remnant of her former life, surfaced in Terra's mind. "Don't you think we should be married?" she said, the question sounding almost like an afterthought, yet carrying a weight of importance that transcended their current state. It was important. Even in undeath, some traditions held a strange, persistent power.

"Of course," he answered, his gaze finally meeting hers, a strange, unsettling mix of affection and something else, something unreadable, lurking within those green depths.

The next few weeks passed in a blur of hurried, unconventional wedding preparations. For Terra, the urgency stemmed from a desire to solidify their bond, to create a semblance of normalcy in their unnatural existence. The ceremony would be small and simple, a clandestine affair held within the shadowed walls of her dwelling. But her white dress, a delicate creation of silk and chiffon she had painstakingly fashioned herself, was stunning, a stark contrast to the decay that surrounded them. Her doom groom, she hoped, would finally see how beautiful she truly was, even in her undead state.

On the day of the wedding, the Bride stood before a cracked and tarnished mirror, ready to be married. Her black hair, carefully combed and curled into styles she remembered from her mortal life, framed her pale face. The white silk and chiffon dress, adorned with delicate fabric flowers all the way down its length, flowed around her like a ghostly shroud, yet held a strange, ethereal beauty. With a steady hand, she applied some light makeup, a habit from her past, and even dared to change the color of her lips from their natural black to a soft pink, hoping to appear more presentable, more... alive.

A moment later, Nathaniel Johnston entered the room. He was still a disconcerting shade of pale purple, the color of a fading bruise. His movements were stiff and unnatural, and the thick black stitches that held him together were starkly visible.

"You really ought to put some makeup on that complexion," Terra said gently, a hint of her former playful nature surfacing. She reached out and pulled up the collar of his ill-fitting suit to try and cover the prominent stitches that encircled his neck. "I'm finally getting married," she said, a strange mix of excitement and melancholy in her voice. "Are you ready for our honeymoon at that castle in Germany?" The idea of escaping this place, of finding some semblance of peace in a new, albeit equally Gothic, setting, appealed to her deeply.

"I am," he answered, his voice still a little rough, but his green eyes held a spark of something akin to anticipation.

Excited despite herself, she leaned in and kissed him lightly on his cold, stitched nose. "Let's go," she said, taking his stiff hand in hers. The ceremony itself was short and sweet, just as they had wanted – a quiet exchange of vows in the dimly lit living room, witnessed only by the shadows and the ghosts of the past.

They embarked on their honeymoon journey in a peaceful, if somewhat dilapidated, rented boat, gliding down a winding river towards their destination in Germany. The scenery was beautiful, the rolling hills and lush greenery a stark contrast to their unnatural existence. They walked up the hill, past a crumbling graveyard with moss-covered stones, to the dark, imposing castle that would be their honeymoon retreat.

They carried their meager luggage up to the third floor of the ancient structure. The room was small but cozy, with a single window overlooking the desolate landscape, a large white bed draped in dust-laden tapestries, and an unlit white candle standing beside it on a rickety bedside table. The Bride dropped her suitcase onto the creaking floorboards and immediately fell onto the soft, surprisingly comfortable bed, a sigh escaping her lips. Just then, a mournful howl echoed through the night – a wolf calling to the moon.

"I love it here," she murmured, turning to Nathaniel. "I love you." She jumped up and hugged her new, reanimated Frankenstein, pressing her cheek against his cold, stitched chest. From somewhere in the distance, seemingly emanating from the graveyard below, they could hear faint, ethereal music, a ghostly melody that seemed to invite them to dance. And so they did, a slow, awkward waltz in the dimly lit room, two undead souls finding a strange comfort in each other's unnatural embrace.

They were not alone in the castle. The old structure was home to a myriad of unseen inhabitants – scurrying mice in the walls, whispers of wind that sounded like ghostly voices, and definitely, undeniably, ghosts, their presence a palpable chill in the air. There was also a caretaker, a gaunt, elderly man with rheumy eyes, who shuffled through the castle halls, tending to its ancient needs. Outside, the chirping of crickets made Bride feel strangely at home, a familiar sound from her past life.

After a surprisingly warm and hearty dinner prepared by the taciturn caretaker, they decided to go for a walk on the castle grounds. The crisp fall air began to blow wildly, swirling fallen leaves around their feet. A sudden, sharp cold chill sent shivers down Terra's unnatural spine, a sensation that made her long for the relative warmth of the castle walls. They talked about their future, their plans for a simple life together, perhaps even returning to her old house in Chicago.

They headed back to their room, the wind whipping around them, carrying the scent of damp earth and decaying leaves. They spent the rest of the day relaxing in the quiet solitude of their newfound marriage, a strange, unsettling peace settling over them.

As Terra lay on a dusty velvet couch in a darker corner of the room, the soft, almost suffocating feel of the fabric lulled her into a light, dreamless sleep. She dreamt of nothing but the vast, star-dusted sky.

Meanwhile, Nathaniel, perhaps seeking a semblance of normalcy or simply driven by a primal urge, headed down to the dark, dank cellar to grab some wine to have with the cheese they had brought. The air in the cellar was heavy with the smell of mildew and old wood. As he peered through the dusty bottles lining the shelves, a man came down the creaking wooden steps. He had light brown hair and a slightly overweight build, an ordinary man who had likely sought refuge in the castle for the night.

Johnston, his reanimated senses perhaps heightened in the darkness, moved silently to the top of the steps and stood to the right of the door, unseen in the shadows. The castle visitor grabbed two bottles of wine, his footsteps echoing in the stillness, and turned to walk back up the stairs. As he looked the other way, a large, pale hand shot out and pushed him with surprising force. The man flailed, his hand instinctively grabbing at the thick black string hanging loosely from Johnston's neck, a grim reminder of his reanimation. But the old, hastily sewn thread snapped under the unexpected strain, and the man tumbled down the steep stairs, his body landing with a sickening thud amidst the shattered remains of the wine bottles.

Johnston, his green eyes now gleaming with a strange, predatory light, descended the stairs. He picked up a jagged piece of broken bottle, the glass sharp and glinting in the dim light filtering from the doorway. With a series of swift, brutal movements, he finished off his victim, five sharp stabs silencing the man's muffled groans. A primal satisfaction, cold and unsettling, washed over him. He dropped the broken bottle and ran silently up the stairs, fleeing out the first door he saw, leaving the lifeless body amidst the spilled wine.

Evening was once again falling on Bride's honeymoon. She had been asleep for hours, a deep, unnatural slumber. When she finally woke, the room was shrouded in darkness. She could hear the muffled sounds of voices coming from downstairs. All the visitors, the other temporary inhabitants of the castle, were gathered in the dining room. She walked down the creaking stairs to join them, but everyone was there except her husband.

A knot of unease tightened in her chest. She ran back up to their room to fetch him, but he wasn't there. She searched the entire floor, then the next, and the next, her footsteps echoing through the empty halls. Still, no sign of Johnston. Not knowing where he was, a growing sense of dread creeping into her undead heart, she went to put on her good black dress, a garment that seemed more fitting for her current mood, and headed down to dinner, hoping he would appear.

Through the long night and the following morning, she waited for Johnston, but he did not return. Impatience and a growing fear gnawed at her. She threw a pillow across the room in frustration. Where was he? she wondered, her thoughts spiraling into dark possibilities. She decided to wait a little longer, trying to convince herself that he was simply out exploring the castle grounds.

The day went on quietly, each hour stretching into an eternity. Bride did her usual things: napped in the dim light of their room, read ancient, dusty books she found in the castle library, enjoyed the eerie grandeur of the castle rooms, and took solitary walks around the desolate area, the wind whispering through the skeletal trees. It was another cold day, so she wore her fur coat, its warmth a small comfort against the growing chill in her heart. There was no sense in sitting around worrying about him more.

When evening came again, she sat by the large stone fireplace in the living room, the flames casting dancing shadows on the walls. The firelight seemed to writhe and twist, looking like demons cavorting in the hearth. She liked being alone for now, the silence a temporary balm to her unease, but the gnawing question of Johnston's whereabouts persisted. While lying on the comfortable, if somewhat musty, velvet couch, she dozed off again, the crackling of the fire her only companion. In the distance, the mournful howl of a pack of wolves echoed through the night, a sound that now seemed less romantic and more ominous.

Knock, knock, knock! A few moments later, a distinct knocking sound started, this time closer. Bang! It was so loud it startled Bride awake. She sat up abruptly, her senses on high alert. "Johnston?" she shouted into the silent room. She got up and searched the immediate area, but there was nothing. The castle was completely dark, save for the flickering firelight, and then a small, insistent rapping started. It sounded like it was coming from beneath the castle, a rhythmic tapping that sent a shiver of unease down her spine.

And so it went on for a while: knock, bang, tap. The annoying, unsettling sounds were suddenly followed by a long, drawn-out moan, a sound that seemed to permeate the very stones of the castle. It was a castle ghost, she realized with a sudden, chilling certainty. The moan was followed by another, even longer and more mournful, and then the knocking and banging started again, a bizarre and terrifying symphony in the darkness.

Fed up with the incessant noise and the growing sense of dread, she grabbed the unlit white candle from their room and a box of matches. With a trembling hand, she lit the candle, the small flame casting flickering shadows on the walls, and left the room, determined to follow the source of the disturbing sounds. She descended the creaking stairs, the candlelight illuminating the dusty banisters and cobweb-laden corners, and headed towards the dark, dank wine cellar, the source of the initial noises.

As she stepped down the last few cellar steps, the flickering light illuminated a gruesome sight. Johnston's victim lay sprawled on the cold stone floor in a growing pool of dark blood! Her mouth fell open in a silent scream, her eyes wide with horror. And there, clutched in the dead man's stiffening fingertips, lay a piece of Johnston's thick black thread. It all made sense now – the strange noises, his disappearance, the cold, predatory look in his eyes.

She stumbled back up the stairs, a strangled scream finally escaping her lips. The gaunt caretaker, who had been sweeping the main hall, started at the sound and rushed towards her, his rheumy eyes widening with alarm. "There's a murdered body in the cellar!" she gasped, her voice shaking uncontrollably. "Call the police!"

The caretaker, his face pale with shock, ran downstairs with a few of the other bewildered castle guests to see for themselves. Terra, her legs feeling like lead, followed them. A collective gasp filled the cellar as they took in the horrifying scene. "It was my husband," Terra whispered, pointing to the black thread in the dead man's hand. "Look at the black thread."

"We'll call the police immediately," the caretaker said, his voice trembling.

Terra, feeling sick to her stomach and a wave of nausea washing over her, ran back up to their room and began to frantically pack her meager belongings. When she came back down the stairs, the sound of sirens wailed in the distance, growing louder as the police arrived. She approached one of the uniformed officers, her face pale and drawn. "I... I didn't see anything happen. It was my husband... he's been missing since last night. The... the man downstairs is holding a piece of his thread."

"We'll take it for evidence, ma'am," the officer said, his expression grim.

"Can you... can you give me a ride out of here? To a Bed and Breakfast or something?" she asked, her voice barely a whisper.

"Okay, ma'am. Grab your suitcases and come with me."

She followed him to the police car, her mind reeling from the horrifying discovery. They got in, and as they drove away from the ominous castle, she made a simple request. "Somewhere quiet," she murmured.

He nodded understandingly, and they drove in silence for a while. As they approached a cozy-looking countryside Bed and Breakfast, the police radio crackled to life. "Officer Davies, we have a report of three more bodies found in Darmstadt. All of them... all of them were found with a piece of black thread clutched in their hands."

The car screeched to a halt.

"That's him," Terra whispered, her voice filled with a chilling certainty. She reached for her suitcases.

"Go check in, ma'am. I'll be back to check on you soon," Officer Davies said, his eyes troubled.

Terra got a small but comfortable room at the Bed and Breakfast. It was late, and exhaustion washed over her. She went straight to bed, her dreams filled with a strange mix of beautiful German grottos and the faint, persistent hope of finding a new, less monstrous love someday. Maybe, just maybe, she would even find a way to be truly alive again.

At 9 a.m., she woke to a gentle knock on the door. A wave of fear washed over her, and she instinctively grabbed the heavy iron fireplace poker beside the hearth. "Room service," a cheerful voice called from the other side of the door.

She dropped the poker with a clatter and cautiously opened the door. A friendly-faced young man wheeled in a trolley laden with warm scrambled eggs, crispy bacon, and a steaming pot of coffee. "Thank you," she said, her voice still a little shaky.

While she was eating, there was another knock on the door. It was Officer Davies. He came in and sat down in the armchair by the window, his expression serious. "We still haven't found him, Ms. Green... or should I say, Ms. Johnston. He may strike again."

"I have an idea," she said, taking a tentative sip of her coffee. "I left his suitcases at the castle. He might be coming back for them. Let's go there, and I'll wait for him. You can be nearby, ready to intervene. Come back when I signal, and you can get him." She took a deep breath, trying to project an air of calm and normalcy, a stark contrast to the undead being she truly was.

"Okay," he said, his eyes thoughtful. "Finish up, and let's go."

Terra did as he suggested, quickly finishing her breakfast. She grabbed her wallet and put on a pair of sturdy walking shoes. As they rode back to the ominous castle in the police car, she turned to Officer Davies, a strange mix of fear and determination in her eyes.

"I have something to tell you," she said, her voice low. "Please... don't laugh. I'm Terra Johnston. I was Frankenstein's fiance, but I decided to marry Nathan instead. I... I brought him back to life, like Frankenstein did, so we could be together. I sewed him back together quickly, with thick black thread first. He's... he's a monster from Chicago."

Officer Davies glanced at her, his expression unreadable. "Ms. Johnston," he said slowly, "you're saying your husband is...?"

"Undead," she finished for him. "Reanimated. Just like Frankenstein's monster."

The police officer remained silent. He stared at her for a long moment, his gaze unwavering. The silence in the car stretched, thick with disbelief and the surreal nature of her confession. Finally, he sighed, a sound that held a mixture of weariness and a dawning sense that perhaps, in this strange case, the unbelievable might just be true.

"Okay," he said slowly, rubbing his temples. "Let's just... process that for a moment. You reanimated your deceased husband?"

"Yes," Terra affirmed, her voice firm despite the tremor in her hands. "With electricity. Like Frankenstein did."

Officer Davies shook his head, a small, disbelieving chuckle escaping his lips. "Right. Well, in that case," he continued, his tone shifting to a more pragmatic one, "you'll need pepper spray, staying in there alone. Bring your phone. What will your signal be?"

"I don't know," Terra admitted, feeling a surge of anxiety. "I'll... I'll scream. Loudly." It seemed like the most straightforward, albeit terrifying, option.

"Are you sure he was really dead?" Officer Davies asked, his eyes searching hers.

"Yes," Terra said, a grim certainty in her voice. "I dug him up myself."

When they arrived back at the imposing castle, a sense of foreboding hung heavy in the air. Nathaniel's luggage was still in their room, a silent testament to his interrupted honeymoon and his current monstrous state. Terra sat on the edge of the dusty bed while Officer Davies, his expression a mask of professional detachment, dusted for fingerprints, a task that seemed almost absurd given the circumstances.

"This was a mistake," Terra murmured, her voice barely audible. The weight of her actions, the horrifying consequences of her desperate attempt to reclaim her lost love, pressed down on her. Time ticked by slowly, each minute stretching into an eternity. The castle remained silent, devoid of any sign of Johnston. A strange sense of false calm settled over Terra, a lull before the storm. Officer Davies, after completing his cursory examination, left the room, promising to be nearby.

A castle employee, a woman in a faded blue maid uniform with a crisp white apron, entered the room quietly. "Would you like some warm tea, madam?" she asked, her voice soft and polite, a stark contrast to the macabre events that had unfolded within these walls.

"Yes, that would be good," Terra replied, her voice weary. The normalcy of the offer was strangely comforting.

While Terra sipped her tea, Officer Davies cautiously made his way down the creaking cellar steps to the scene of the crime. The air in the cellar was cold and damp, still heavy with the coppery scent of blood. Broken glass crunched under his shoes as he surveyed the gruesome scene, his flashlight beam cutting through the darkness.

Upstairs, Terra felt a sudden prickling sensation on the back of her neck. The air in the room seemed to grow colder. She took another slow sip of her tea, trying to ignore the growing unease. Then, a shadow fell across the doorway.

Nathaniel crept into the room like a hungry wolf, his movements silent and predatory. The green eyes that had once held affection now held a blank, terrifying zombie stare. He lunged towards her with unnatural speed.

Terror surged through Terra. She reacted instinctively, grabbing Johnston's heavy suitcase from the floor and throwing it with all her might at his head. It connected with a sickening thud, momentarily staggering him. Before he could recover, she grabbed a large, ornate vase from the bedside table and hurled it next. It shattered against the wall behind him, the ceramic shards scattering across the floor. He stumbled, hitting the ground with a heavy thud.

Her hand instinctively went to her pocket, finding the small can of pepper spray Officer Davies had given her. With a trembling finger, she aimed and sprayed a generous burst into Johnston's vacant green eyes. He roared in pain and confusion, clawing at his face. Fueled by a surge of adrenaline and a bitter sense of betrayal, she angrily slapped his pale, stitched face. This was not her beloved Nathaniel. This was a monster.

"How do you stand the sight of yourself?" she hissed, her voice filled with disgust and a strange, unexpected pity for the creature he had become.

He seemed oblivious to her words, his movements jerky and uncoordinated. He sat up, and a long, tattered piece of black string hung loosely from his neck, a grotesque reminder of her hasty handiwork. A desperate idea sparked in Terra's mind. She lunged forward and grabbed the loose end of the thread, pulling it with all her strength.

The thick black thread slid out, inch by agonizing inch. Nathaniel thrashed and groaned, his body convulsing. Then, with a sickening lurch, his head rolled off his shoulders and landed with a dull thud at his feet, his vacant green eyes staring up at her.

"Help!" Terra screamed, her voice raw with terror and revulsion.

Officer Davies burst into the room, his gun drawn. He stopped short, his eyes widening at the horrifying scene before him. Terra stood there, trembling, the long black thread clutched in her hand, the same thread that had been found clutched in the hands of Johnston's victims. Her can of mace lay on the floor beside her. In a final act of horrified desperation, she yanked off Johnston's arms and legs, the unnatural joins tearing with a sickening sound.

Officer Davies, his face pale, holstered his weapon. He went to his car and returned with a large black body bag. Wordlessly, he and Terra placed the dismembered remains of Nathaniel Johnston inside. As he drove her back to the Bed and Breakfast, the gruesome contents of the body bag rolled ominously in the trunk.

"You are going to burn him, aren't you?" Terra asked, her voice flat and devoid of emotion.

"Of course," he answered grimly, his eyes fixed on the road ahead.

Back in the quiet comfort of her room at the Bed and Breakfast, Terra sank into a soft armchair, the familiar surroundings a small balm to her shattered nerves. "Room sweet room," she murmured, the phrase taking on a new, poignant meaning. She wanted to stay here for a while, to try and piece together the fragments of her broken existence. The fire crackled merrily in the hearth, casting a warm glow on the room as she ate a bowl of hot stew, the simple act of nourishment a small step back towards normalcy.

Just then, the phone rang, its shrill sound cutting through the quiet. It was Officer Davies. "Just so you know, Ms. Johnston," he said, his voice firm, "he was incinerated at the crematory. He won't be back."

"So," Terra said softly, a hint of relief in her voice, "you do believe me."

"Of course," he responded, a hint of understanding in his tone.

Her disastrous honeymoon had inadvertently turned into a solitary German vacation. With a newfound sense of freedom, albeit tinged with sadness, Terra decided to explore the beautiful German countryside. She visited the stunning grottos, marveled at the vibrant flowers scattered across the landscape, and found a strange sense of peace in the quiet solitude. The darkness no longer held the same terror for her, not after facing the true horror that had resided in the reanimated form of her lost love. Seeing Nathaniel creep into her room with that blank, murderous stare had been more terrifying than any shadow. In a strange, twisted way, it was the best vacation ever, a journey of self-discovery after a second, even more bizarre death. Getting back home, whenever that might be, felt like a genuine new start for her strange, unnaturally prolonged life after death.

Love On All Hallows' Eve

The cold fall air blew over Terra's face and through her long, curly, black hair. It was the night before Halloween and Terra's mind drifted away. She was on one of her late-night strolls through the local graveyard. Sitting on a grassy mound she watched the blood moon turn slightly red. This part of Chicago was peaceful and restful. No city noise to disturb anyone.

Fall leaves blew and circled her a few times then left. Her black lips glistened as she smiled in the night.The reddish moon interested her, and she wanted to know more. Why was Samhain so interesting? She didn't know anything about it but wanted to. She would start by studying the moon. The night was spent reading a book about it and the fall solstice. It was 1979 and little did she know Halloween was approaching at midnight. Heading back home she began to feel alone. Going out at night made her feel lonely. She did not know anyone. Her new name was Johnston, but she was not married to that new monster husband she made long before he was destroyed for being evil.She reflected on her living time with him sometimes.She wanted to meet people. As the sun gave a hint of sunlight it was time to sleep at home. She wondered if Frankenstein would ever come back to claim her. Probably not.

On Halloween night Terra sat quietly in her room. Creepy cackling and bubbling could be heard, then footsteps. She went outside and saw nothing. The full moon lit the area well. Curiously she headed to the graveyard and sat on a large tombstone. Crickets chirped and fireflies flew, but that was all. It was time to go past the graveyard. Walking near a road she heard voices. Two young men were chatting and a little drunk because they were coming from a

Halloween costume party. One was dressed as a vampire with teeth, dark slick hair, pale skin, and a dark cape. The other, his close friend, was Frankenstein. They looked very good, tall and dark.

Terra approached them.

"It's back that way," Frankenstein said pointing in the direction of the party.

"I don't need that info from you anymore," Terra said to what she thought was her ex but was wrong. The green makeup concealed his true identity. She walked over to the vampire and put her arm through his. "What part of this country are you from?"

"South of Chicago," the vampire replied.

"I'm Terra. I'm the bride of Frankenstein or was. Care to get a drink?" she asked the vampire only speaking to him and refusing to acknowledge the guy dressed as Frankenstein. She wanted to make him jealous, but it was unlikely because he didn't know her and wasn't really Frankenstein. He didn't seem to care and gave Terra Belinda a mad look.

"Why not." The phony vampire's teeth sparkled. He smirked at Frankenstein. "I'm Dracula," he said to her with a Transylvanian accent. He looked so handsome in the dark. Terra didn't look so bad herself.

"I'll see ya later," Dracula said to Frankenstein. They were off to have a romantic drink.

Terra and Dracula had their drink quickly. They only had one shot. "Can we do it again some time?" she asked.

"Yes," the vampire said. "I'll come by and get you this Friday evening. We'll have a candlelit dinner at my house. Let's go to that party I mentioned. Frankenstein, my friend is a deadbeat. He wouldn't go."

"That sounds lovely! Alright."

He began walking her there. "Don't hate my friend Frankenstein. He can be nice."

"I know. I was engaged to him once. Didn't know him well. You, I'd like to get to know," she said confused and started to realize her fiance Frankenstein wasn't the same as Bobby's friend.

"I will see you then." He kissed her on the cheek and stepped back as she entered the party. It was thrown by one of Bobby's parents' friends from high school and everyone was invited. There were cupcakes and plenty of music for them to dance to. On the left in a dark corner was a haunted house they could walk through. It was awesome! They danced together around orange twinkle lights.

Bobby's friend Frankenstein entered the room. He had followed them. He raised his arms at Bobby, so he explained himself. "I'm going to go out with this girl again. I like her," Dracula said to

Frankenstein. I have a stomachache." He was dancing and twisting so he stopped and went to sit down.

"There's a haunted house." He pointed. "Let's go in."

"I didn't know the party would be this cool! Just don't let her find out you're not a vampire. Why

does she believe we are monsters?" His friend Tim shrugged his shoulders not getting it.

"I don't know. Good costumes," he said shrugging in response.

"Watch her. I think she's weird."

"Pretty, but weird. She won't find out. I'll only come out at night," the vampire swore. "How is it you're not sick too?"

"I hold my liquor," the green one answered, and they both laughed.

"I need to prepare for our Friday dinner. Do you know where I can get a hearse and a coffin? And I want to shop at one of those Halloween stores. They are probably having clearance sales." Bobby said as they entered the haunted house. It was pitch dark except for the doorway.

"I know a company. I'll ask if we can borrow or rent," Frankenstein said hatefully. "How long can this go on for?"

"I don't know. I'll wait until she loves me and cares for me too much to get mad. Then I'll tell her

I'm not a vampire."

"I mean this tunnel. OK, I'll get started on that hearse. It ought to be fun driving it."

"Ya, we'll take it first and cruise in it." He laughed to himself. "What will people think?" Bobby chuckled to himself. As he did a man dressed as a vintage werewolf came walking towards them and they ran into the next room and locked the door. It had some light only a little yellow one near a dummy of a dead body getting an autopsy. They were in a fake morgue. A fake scream sounded from outside the room. Bobby rolled his eyes and opened the door. It was Terra. The scream had been her.

"What are you guys doing in here?" she asked.

"Nothing, going through the haunted house," Bobby said to cover up the fact they ran. "Why did you scream?"

"The wolfman came at me," she said smiling. "Let's go."

"I'm not going anywhere." Bobby said as the three of them went towards the end of the hall. A chainsaw sounded and they ran to a door that led them to the dance floor. Terra ignored the fact the house was over and began dancing. Her lightweight white dress flowed with her turns and people grabbed handfuls of candy. The guys decided they needed to get some quick. The night was too much fun and they hung out but did not go back into the haunted house.

***

Dracula, aka Bobby, was finishing setting up the dining area. The table was set with metal plates, red candles, and glass goblets. The room was dark and dusty. His friend, Frankenstein, rented a hearse for him, and he kept a coffin in one of his rooms. The creepiest room in the house. The hearse was to pick her up in. There were small white candles in the bathroom, they were all around the house.

He had prepared a couple days ahead of time and still needed to figure out what to have for dinner. There would be red wine. He would be in costume of course to fool her. He wanted her to think he was a real vampire. "Don't call me on this date night," he told Frankenstein.

"Let's cruise in that hearse," Frankenstein suggested.

"Won't people stare?" Dracula asked.

"Ya Drac, we'll stay away from town. You know what would be cool? To park it by the graveyard." Tim looked excited about the idea.

"Are you sure there's no body in it anymore?" Drac looked afraid.

"Ya. Besides, you need to practice driving it." Frankenstein was the one who rented and drove it there. He handed Drac the keys. "We'll take the back roads to the lake. You walk to the store and buy dinner. Come evening we'll drive it to the graveyard."

Drac nodded without a choice. He tried to stay away from cars. Although the back window curtains covered too much. They found a small grocery store near the lake, and Drac shopped for his dark date night. Night came closing in and they headed back to the Chicago graveyard.

"Looks like you're getting the hang of this car." Tim watched him drive it well.

Drac nodded. "Is there anything I missed for our dinner?"

"Let's go cruise to the Halloween shop to see if they have anything good left. Something to add to your vampire look. Like fake blood. Then we'll drive through the graveyard."

As they drove that way the full moon still hung overhead, but not very bright. The first evening stars were starting to show. After purchasing a few items, they parked in the graveyard. Only one other car drove by. An owl hooted from a tree. Drac turned on the headlights, and they got out to walk around. Dark clouds covered the moon and suddenly Drac fell into a shallow empty grave! He stood up and glanced at the scrape on his arm. Immediately, his eyes went to the round gravestone. It read Terra Belinda Green, Beloved daughter June 11, 1898 - September 2, 1928. They knew who it was. Drac took a quick deep breath, and Frankenstein pulled him out of the ditch. They ran to the car and took off fast.

When they got home, they locked the door and turned on the lights. Very upset, he knocked over his vampire decorations. "I didn't know she was dead! What should I do?"

"I'm not sure." His friend looked puzzled.

"Should I go on the date? If I cancel she'll get mad and attack."

"This is ridiculous," Tim said.

"And you know what? I don't like that hearse. But she's got long black nails and she's so beautiful.

Beauty never dies."

"I have a plan," Tim that was Frankenstein said. "Cook her dinner tomorrow. You go get her, and I'll hide in the basement with the door locked. I'll have a rope and weapons to keep us safe. After you eat, keep the house dark and take her to the living room. I'll sneak out, whack her with a bat, and tie her up. She'll realize we're fake monsters then, so we'll take her to the forest and leave her there.

Maybe the real Frankenstein will come get her."

"To kill her?" Drac asked.

"You can't kill something that's dead. I hate to say this, but we'll see what happens. We won't drop her off nearby, ok. And we do need to kill her. Let's get ready for her, to cook her as the dinner." "Alright Tim." The plan was set. Tim spent the night, and he was ready. They hung out in the basement with the weapons. He was there for his friend Bobby. If he stood her up, they didn't know what she would do. She lived close in a creepy, gray, gloomy house.

When the next evening came, Bobby got into his vampire costume. His meat was crackling in the oven and his potatoes were baking. "While I'm out picking her up, light the candles on the dining room table, bathroom, and coffin room."

Tim did not argue. He was there to help. "I'll leave the dinner in the oven to keep it warm. Are you ready to drive the hearse?"

"No," Bobby answered nervously. Then he chuckled. "Well, there's plenty of room to shove her in the back. I'll get gas now."

"Right." It was set, but no creepy music. Bobby didn't like it.

The minute Bobby left the house Tim lit the candles then ran into the basement and locked the door. He had a lantern down there and could hear the cricket's chirp.

When Bobby got to Terra's house after filling the tank with a gas can, he rang the doorbell. She came out dressed nicely and said, "Hi."

"Hi. If you're ready let's go." He walked to the hearse and opened the door for her. She stared at it then got in.

"How far do you live?" she asked.

"Just ten minutes away," he answered.

"This is nice," she looked around comfortably.

"I don't usually drive. I'm not out during the day." He started to drive trying to sound like he was really a vampire.

"I am not either." She didn't go out during the day usually so that no one would figure out she was undead. That was Dr. Frankenstein's fault.

"I hope you like rare meat and wine."

"I do," she said pleased. "With a lot of blood."

"Me too." He lied. "Hopefully we'll do this often. Do you want to go for a walk after dinner?" He couldn't keep his eyes on the road.

"Mhmm," she nicely accepted.

When they got to the house it was dark. "We're finally here." He owned a white two-story house. With only grass and a dead tree in the yard. They headed for the door.

When they entered, it was dark with candles lit. "What time is dinner?" she asked.

"I'm keeping it warm in the oven. We can eat now. This is a very big house. I have a couple of guest rooms and my bedroom."

She walked around looking in the rooms, then last she entered his bedroom. There was a large dark wood coffin that was open. It had red velvet inside. "Do you like red?" she asked loud enough for him to hear in the kitchen.

"Yes, I love it."

She stood alone and approached the coffin. She went inside and laid down. Rubbing her hands on the velvet she closed her eyes. It was comfortable. To try it out Terra closed the coffin. It was dark. Not for the living. She did have a grave, but never knew what it was like. There would be no returning there. Life and the afterlife were too precious.

It made her think, remember, and want to talk to family. But all the family she knew were gone. She drifted away liking the coffin.

"Terra," Dracula called.

Quickly she got up and ran to the dining room. The Gothic vampire table was cool. Her eyes widened. Dinner looked great!

He poured red wine into her goblet then kissed her. "You look dazzling," he said.

"Thank you." Her purple dress with black heels was perfect for the night. There was little conversation. They mostly ate as they were so hungry. Her eyes sparkled brownish black in the candlelight. It was magical.

"Would you like to go for a walk after dinner soon?"

"Sure," Terra really liked the idea. "How about through the forest?"

"Okay, how did you know Frankenstein?"

"I'm the bride of Frankenstein, though we never married. We were engaged, and he went on a killing rampage and then ran into the forest. I was married once. He was also a zombie, brought to life by galvanism. We weren't together for even a week during the honeymoon. My last name became

Johnston."

"This is good. I don't get too many good meals," she added.

"I'm glad you like it. How did you like the hearse?"

"It was different. I like your coffin. I must get one," she said lying about the hearse but not the coffin. The coffin was comfortable but the hearse, a nightmare.

"You should. And next time we won't come here in the hearse. To be honest, I don't like it either." Bobby watched her finish. There was not a single light on in the house. "Are you ready for a walk?"

"Ya, sure."

He kicked himself.

"What?" She looked at him funny.

"I don't have dessert. What do zombies eat, brains?" he asked.

"Yes. We can go get it. Not brains. I'm not that kind of zombie."

Bobby stood to go on the walk. "Don't you want to blow out the candles first? I noticed you left them lit when you came to get me. You could burn down your house."

"Yes of course." He blew all of them out. There were so many she helped him. They went outside for a night walk. It seemed romantic, especially when there were no words. Wind blew through the bare trees. He gave her his jacket to wear. Clop clop, there was the sound of loud footsteps in the forest. Terra jumped. "He comes."

"Who comes?"

"Frankenstein."

"I thought he was gone." He turned and saw a partially broken branch blowing and hitting itself. That was the real cause of the noise.

"One day he will come for me."

"But you wouldn't marry him?" Bobby asked.

"That was a nice walk. Let's watch a romance movie. Do you have a name besides Dracula?" Surprise, she was intelligent.

"I do go by Dracula, but my real name's Bobby. I'm not the real Vladimir Dracula." He took a deep breath. "I'm glad we met. We will do this again soon. I hope." He really liked her and did not want her to go. He did not know how to deal with the fact she was dead. "I have to tell you something," he wanted to save her. He liked her so he had a change of heart.

Suddenly she was whacked in the head and fell to the floor. Her head was sore and weak, so she closed her eyes. Tim began to tie her up. He had a knife in his belt. It was too late to save her, and he went along with the plan.

"I told her my name was Bobby."

He then told Terra, "This is your Frankenstein. He is not a monster like you." He really seemed to hate monsters.

She recognized him. Terra jerked to hit him but couldn't with her hands behind her back. Tim slapped her a few times.

"I want her now," Bobby yelled at him. He didn't want to hurt her, he wanted to be with her.

"What do you mean? You guys planned this?" she whined.

Bobby nodded. "Why did you think we were monsters?"

"I didn't know at first! It's my world," she shouted.

He glared back at her. They grabbed her hands and feet. Bobby noticed she didn't breathe much.

"Not in the hearse," he complained because he hated it.

Tim laughed. "There's more room, it's harder to see in, and people won't ask questions." He put her in the hearses. They drove for almost two hours to the woods. Tim got out and tied her to a tree.

"There you go, freak." He kicked dirt at her feet, and she growled at him.

"You think she can find her way back?" Bob asked.

"It would take many hours," Tim said, aggravated. He grabbed his knife and slashed her chest. They left to sit and drink in the dark cold stream there. "Why don't dead people sleep?" Tim yelled at her so she would hear.

"Maybe because they are tired of you!" Terra looked up to dark gray clouds moving. The wind began blowing harder. Leaves passed them as it darkened, and clouds covered the moon. She twisted in her ropes. Thunder sounded close by, and a light fall rain began.

Lightning struck the tree she was tied to! It fried the ropes, and she pulled them free as the broken tree fell. Approaching Tim, she wrapped her rope around his neck and choked him! "You want to be real monsters?" It was an unwanted invitation. With her free hand she hit Bobby, and he fell in the water. In an instant she had Tim's knife and killed them both.

Rain fell harder and spread blood all over the stream. She took the car keys and opened the hearse.

The men were dragged and put in the back. She covered them with a blanket so it would appear the bodies were being transported. She drove them to Frankenstein's lab soaking wet. It was still raining and almost midnight, so the back curtain was pulled down at the back of the hearse and she went inside. Maybe she didn't have to kill them, but she wasn't sure. Who knew what they would actually do. Being already dead she feared a second death.

In the morning, they both were wheeled into the galvanism room and were brought to life by large amounts of electricity traveling over their bodies. They twitched as blue light covered them. Their eyes opened! They looked dirty and undead. For a moment

Terra worried they would get revenge, but she had just gotten hers. Tim stood up and walked away now transformed into a Frankenstein. The other one followed, and she let them wander out the door. Terra quickly ran and locked it.

***

The hunter Rusty Cortez held his shotgun as he watched the fish in the stream. He hadn't caught much, just a deer and was thinking about fishing instead. There was a bait and tackle shop fifteen minutes down the road. Then he heard it. What was it? Something strange dragging. He loaded it and pointed his gun at the noise. With blank stares, they came out of the woods walking straight towards him. He opened fire, and they kept coming. It was Bobby and Tim. He reloaded then hit Bobby between the eyes when he realized he was undead. He stared at the costume corpse. Tim bit his arm and locked his jaw there. The hunter shot him too and his arm stung greatly.

He wanted to call for help but didn't know if they would believe him. He buried them feet away from the trees and stream so they wouldn't be found. He couldn't prove they were already dead when he shot them. He cleaned his arm in the stream and left for home. He looked back at the woods driving away as evening crept in.

When he got home, he bandaged his arm and went straight to bed. His wife Rose was already asleep. She was a psychic, and he hoped she wouldn't sense everything that happened. It was hard being married to a psychic. She always wanted to read and know his actions away from her.

As she slept soundly and turned over, her rose gold hair fell around her shoulders. She was different, a special person. That's why he married her. They were married five years and lived in a cozy two-story home built in 1942, but still had no children. He felt sick to his stomach and was wondering how he would explain it in the morning.

"Rusty," his wife called him. She had made eggs benedict with avocado toast. His favorite. When she went up to fetch him, he was lying pale and sweaty. He was sick. "What did you do out there?" she asked in a suspicious voice.

"I was bit by something. Maybe bacteria got in, and now I'm sick." She saw the big bloody bandage.

"Go properly wash it and I'll make you soup." He nodded and closed his eyes. Her light blue eyes were trusted by people. She left him to sleep.

By the time he woke she had chicken soup made, aspirin, and was wiping his forehead. "I need to go to work." She worked in a local psychic reading shop. "I'll call the doctor when I get home." She kissed his forehead. It was hot. The zombie bite gave him an infection.

As she walked away, he grabbed the aspirin and took it. He heard the front door slam and stared at the ceiling thinking of his wife. He remembered meeting her. She wore a red flower in her hair and had naturally red lips. He was working on a construction site, and she was telling fortunes at home with a crystal ball and tarot cards. When he saw how she cared for her customers personally and loved animals, he knew he wanted to marry her kind heart. He got her a ruby heart necklace and one evening came knocking with a ring. When he entered he said, "Hi dear. I've seen how kind you are, and we've been dating for a few months.."

"You are proposing. I see us married." She looked down, and he laughed. He hugged her with gladness in his heart. She had made a beautiful bride. With long white satin and yellow daisies. When he bought honeymoon tickets to the Bahamas she knew. "We're going to the Bahamas!" She lept with joy. She became Rose Cortez. They were meant to be.

***

The mirror shook on the wall. There was fog, and it came from the mirror on the floor. It was a gold framed mirror that hung in her bedroom. When she got up that morning, she picked it up.

"Dracula won't see his reflection in this mirror." And she hung it back up.

Terra wondered when the Frankenstein's she created would come back. "Where are the spooky twins?" She wanted to go back and visit her old home she lived in as a child. She grew up there and it was hers in 1900. The house was built in 1840. It would have been nice to see an old face she knew in life. It was too lonely. It would be good to see the old part of town she lived in and maybe a museum. After putting something warm on she went to grab her jacket and found her mirror on the floor again. Was something amiss? Was it really there again? She picked it up feeling like she had done something to deserve it.

Terra believed in evil but didn't know anything about it. There was the knowledge she killed her boyfriend and his friend, but it was in self-defense. She saw the nail on the wall where the mirror hung, and it was fine. After hanging it up again, she went on with her day.

***

When she approached her old mansion in the hearse, she tried to remember her life there, but it was interrupted by the for rent sign in the yard. Terra took down the number. It was the place she got sick and died. It was the place where she had her baby Tyra, and it was taken from her because she was accused of neglect. It looked very old and dusty. Over a hundred years. It was her home, and she loved it. No doubt it needed work.

Unable to get in she looked through each window. It looked almost the same. Were her belongings still in there? She saw candle holders and the old fireplace. It looked Victorian and was so full of memories. Mostly because of growing up there and her parents. Staring at the dust through the window, she called the realtor and told them she wanted to rent it.

It was at a good price because it needed work. "I used to l," she stopped herself from saying she lived there. "I'm coming right now to get the keys." She planned to sell the hearse. She would sell the place she lived in and considered going into Bobby's house and selling his stuff. "Those jerks," she said to herself excitedly speeding to the realtors. Driving by, she noticed Rose's psychic shop. Interested, she made a mental note of it.

Just then the radio turned on. She then hit a pothole and the curtains closed. The radio was not clear, but staticky. Then she heard someone call her name. She didn't know what to do and pulled over. As she got out an old song played loudly. Terra ran the rest of the way to the realtors. Going in she wanted to believe that it was Bobby and Sam. It really was. Everything went perfectly and she got the keys. There was no ride to the mansion or home, so she had to go back and get the hearse.

Arriving back at the mansion she decided to hire people to help her clean it. If she left before nightfall the hearse shouldn't be a problem. She fell asleep on the couch.

That night at home she had not started packing yet. She just started throwing out junk and getting out boxes. Waking at night she saw it. The mist in the mirror. Then a white ghostly male face.

Strangely it did not look at her. It was Tim. The mirror floated off the wall and landed on her bed.

Terra wanted to pick it up and get rid of it, but she was afraid. A mist came out of the mirror, and she kicked it out of the room, then out the door and she picked it up. It then shook hard and fell to the cement into a hundred pieces. The white ghost flew out and went into Terra's house. She ran inside to find it. When passing the bathroom, he appeared. Terra frowned knowing she couldn't take it outside and drop the mirror. She shut the bathroom door and went into the bedroom. Its voice called, "Terra." As the night went by things could be heard dropping in the bathroom. Was he a poltergeist?

Not knowing the answers to her questions, the next morning she began packing. Afterwards, the house needed to be cleaned. The same Realtor she rented from was going to sell her house, and she left the house very dirty.

The maids were hired to clean her old mansion starting immediately. It was a lot of work, and she needed a break, so she went to get lunch and go see that psychic place that she passed the day before. As she entered there were crystals, candles, and a velvet covered table! Rose Cortez approached her and said, "Would you like a reading?"

"Ya, and I need to talk about a ghost that is in my house."

"I understand. Go on."

"It recently started. I've seen him in the mirror." They sat at the table. "My car radio turned on, and my mirror fell. I accidentally dropped it outside when it shook hard, and the ghost flew into my bathroom mirror."

"I should start my reading here. I can use my crystal ball and tarot cards. These mirror ghosts. Do you know who they are?" Rose asked.

Bobby, a guy I was dating and his friend Tim. They were mean to me alive."

"The mirror is how they get into the house. It's a portal." Rose lit candles.

"I just purchased my old mansion as a rental. So, I'm moving away."

"You want to get rid of it now. It is angry and may try to follow you." Rose grabbed a jar. "This is a spirit jar. Grab plenty of hollowed dirt from a church or graveyard. Place a candle in the middle." Rose handed her a small white candle. "Light it and place the jar in the middle of the room. You leave and let the candle completely burn itself down. The flame will draw the ghost into the jar. Then close it, take it to the church or graveyard, bury it and cover it with salt. Those grounds are hollowed, and it is where the jar needs to be."

"Thank you," Terra said. Rose pushed the jar and matches to her. "Are they poltergeists?"

Rose looked into her crystal ball seeing everything that happened between her husband and the two ghosts. "No just two mean and evil ghosts." She looked very concerned. "My husband is sick. They were zombies and bit him. I don't know what to do with him." She handed Terra her business card. "Call me if it gets out of hand. That must mean my husband killed them and buried them somewhere.

It would be hard to find the spot out in the woods."

"Looks like we both have a dilemma. Thanks so much for your help. I'm going to buy a cross to hang in my bedroom. I'll call you," Terra said, and she took her spirit jar.

"I hope to hear from you."

Terra left not wanting her to read any more. It was her that killed and brought back the

Frankenstein's. She was the reason Rose's husband was sick. Also, Terra was dead. How would she ever come back to life?

After getting home the cross was hung, but she did not feel like cleaning. Instead, every mirror in the house was thrown out, except the bathroom.

***

"I know what bit you," Rose said to Rusty. His eyes got big.

"They attacked me."

"Now I have to find the bodies." Rose was serious.

"I'll tell you where they are. Can we burn them?"

"There's a crime that hasn't been reported. A woman named Terra came in today. Reading her I saw that she killed them after they tied her up. I didn't say anything. They are haunting her."

"Will I live?" He wasn't sure she knew the answer. She wasn't a doctor, but a zombie bite meant something bad.

"No, and you will be like them except without electricity to bring you to life."

"I buried them because I couldn't explain it. I don't think I will become a zombie."

"You have a psychic's word to back you up. We will dig them up and leave them to be found. Don't you want justice? They've killed you." Rose thought her husband was dying of the zombie virus. Nothing had been diagnosed.

"Yes, with maybe an anonymous report." He sat up.

"Terra killed them in self-defense. It was not your fault they died. They were already gone."

"She did us all a favor," he said in pain.

"Are you coming to get the bodies?" she asked.

"I'll take you there." He got up a little weak. It took the day to take care of the bodies. When they got home, they passed out. Rose did not sleep by Rusty that night, but behind a locked door.

***

Terra dreaded nightfall now. It wasn't the only bathroom, so she spent her time packing it up and putting the boxes in her other bathroom. When she went to shut the door, she saw Sam's face in the mirror. Immediately Terra went to the church and scooped an inch and a half of dirt into the spirit jar. No one saw her.

After going to the haunted bathroom, she put the candle inside and lit it. Terra placed it in the middle of the floor. She then tried to go on with her day packing.

They had just started cleaning the mansion when Terra dropped off boxes. In that bathroom she stared at her reflection. No ghosts there. Two people worked to clean, and she went to her old bedroom. It needed a bed.

***

Lying awake that night the Cortez's woke up. "There is one way to survive that bite I didn't want to
mention, amputation."

"I think it's too late."

"Maybe there's no virus, but an infection. I can tell because you have not turned into a zombie.

They came back by lightning striking," she said.

"I haven't gotten better."

In the morning when Rose woke up she called Rusty's name and shook him to wake him, but he did not respond. An ambulance was called, and he was taken to the hospital. She was told it was sepsis from the infection. He was not coming home soon.

***

Terra covered the jar with a lid. Heading to the church with salt she arrived and began to dig behind it with a little shovel.

"What are you doing?" A man in a suit asked.

"Burying this jar."

"I don't want that mumbo jumbo near our church. People should come here not worried about disturbance."

"There won't be a disturbance. It's hallowed ground," she insisted.

"Yes, But I don't want that in our yard! There are children here."

She picked it up and took a breath. "I can take it to the graveyard instead."

"I hope that isn't witchcraft," he said about the salt. He was one of the church Pastors and he wasn't happy with her.

She shook her head no and walked away. When getting to the graveyard, she placed the jar in the hole, sprinkled salt, buried it, and then sprinkled more. She placed a large flat rock on top to keep it down.

Terra continued to move without any paranormal disturbance. She was a monster, but trusted God.

Maybe heaven was where she should have been all along. The thought had occurred to her to pray to God to ask him to take her or be allowed some more time on earth. Not being religious during life, she thought about God more after death. Terra did decide to call Rose and let her know it worked.

"My husband is in the hospital from an undead bite. It turns out corpses have dirty teeth. We didn't know how to clean it properly. He has sepsis," Rose said on the phone to Terra.

"Is he going to be okay?"

"We don't know. He is on antibiotics. I've seen him almost every day."

"I would like you to stop by my mansion. I want to make sure where I'm moving is free of ghosts."

"Okay. Would it be fine if I stay the night to be sure? We can do a séance. Just kidding," she laughed.

"Alright. Tomorrow ok?"

"That's fine."

Terra gave her the address and time. She felt anxious about the move and the psychic coming. She hadn't moved in yet but wanted to pack to spend that night. Memories of her childhood there passed her mind. The old building wasn't expensive to rent. Nobody wanted it but it meant everything to Terra.

***

Rose walked through all the rooms. "There are no ghosts here. That's what you thought." The house was still.

"I'm moving in then, today. There's something I didn't tell you. Those ghosts were my fault. I killed them and brought them back by electricity because they were pretending to be monsters to me and wanted to kill me because they knew I was undead."

"I know. You're OK now. Rusty made an anonymous report to the police because they kidnapped you."

"It's their spirits I'm worried about. What if they were dug up? I buried them in the graveyard by the church."

"Would you like another reading?" Rose offered to reassure her.

"No. I'll be fine. There won't be any mirrors in this house. How did you know what happened?" Terra shook from the thought.

"I saw it in the crystal ball. We have to wait until tonight so I can see if any ghosts show themselves."

Terra nodded. When Rose laid down her sleeping bag in the living room Rose said, "I have another bed in the first bedroom in the hall."

"Oh great. Rose immediately headed there. She picked up the phone and made some calls to her shop. Approaching she told her, "This house is beautiful." She liked the spacious mansion.

"Aren't you afraid the ghosts will come tonight?" Terra asked.

"No, you said you got rid of the bad ones. If anything comes we'll just do another spirit jar and get you something for protection like a witch ball."

"Are you into witchcraft?" Terra sat curiously looking over Roses black dress and half-moon ring. Her hair was long, and she wore only black eyeliner.

"Yes, I never wanted to be a witch, but I realized it will help my clients to cast good white spells. I got good at it and let myself become a witch for more power. I may not do it forever." She was worrying about what people thought of her. "Never do a Ouija board here. It will invite spirits in. I'm not even sure we should do a seance. If your dead wouldn't that help you know or see ghosts?" Rose leaned closer to see if Terra smelled of decomposition. She did not and none was present.

"I have never seen a ghost while being this way. Come on. I'll make you lunch."

They both got up and Rose asked, "Do you have to eat?"

"No."

"I called my husband at the hospital, and he says he's sicker. I may have to go see him later."

"That's ok," Terra answered.

"I'll let you know. I can do this." Rose began to make a sandwich she wanted. She ate it as she walked around the house absorbing it more. "What's that side door on the top floor?"

"The attic. It scared me when I was a kid."

"We must go in there," Rose said wide eyed.

Upon opening the door, they saw old store junk and thick dust. "Let's sweep the dust and maybe we could have the seance up here."

"I don't think so. won't that cause more trouble?" Terra asked.

"Come on. You're dead already and I'm a witch. I'll cast a circle of protection. There's nothing to be afraid of. We don't even know if anything will answer. We could call those two you killed to see if they broke free or even Frankenstein if you want. He couldn't still be out there."

"Ok." They began cleaning up and even sprayed a little for spiders. The cover was lifted off the window and sunlight shone in. Terra went to her old toy box with her name spelled in big white letters.

Her toys were still there but dirty. A breeze blew in and the door slammed shut. "What if your husband dies? I am so sorry. I guess I never thought they would hurt anybody."

"I know. Whatever happens it is not your fault. You did what you had to do. You seem alive and I'm sure feel it. You had to protect your life. Rusty should have gone to the doctor sooner." She was trying to forgive, and she did but somehow it was still hard to let go, and thoughts of revenge would pass her mind. She ignored them with no real intention of hurting anyone. For now, they were friends and Rose wouldn't mind staying there.

They finished dusting and moved to a small table with two chairs. When the attic had everything shoved to the side with the floor mostly open and a table just for the seance they decided to have dinner. "I thought you didn't eat," Rose said.

"I don't have to, but I have decided to. I can't taste much either." Terra made spaghetti because it was easy besides adding meatballs and mushrooms. When it was done cooking she went up to get

Rose. Rose had laid a black velvet cover on the table she had found and a big white candle. "I don't know about this."

"It's OK. We'll leave the door open, but it has to be dark. It's evening, we'll eat then see if it's pitch black. When it is we can come up here."

"If we find spirits can we get rid of them?" Terra asked.

"Yes if we are successful. They can be stubborn. This is an old house. Anyone could be here."

Terra ate dinner and relaxed. When night had fallen Rose came to get her. "Let's go."

Up the stairs they went to the attic door. Rose lit the candle and shut the door a little. She joined

Terra's hands. They felt ice cold. "We wish to speak to the dead. Does anyone not living wish to reveal yourself. If you don't do it now, you cannot do it later in a malevolent way when unexpected." Terra watched Rose feeling that she had forgotten Terra was dead. "I am calling the spirits of the dead. Do you have a message good or bad?" When Rose said dead Terra would look at her. She herself was dead and she smiled. Nothing responded.

"I guess there's no one here," Terra added giving up. Ghosts or no ghosts she lived in the house and wanted to live in it. There was a creak outside the door. Rose went to investigate it but when she got to the room it came from nothing was there.

She returned. "Are you trying to make contact?" A child's rocking horse rocked twice in the corner. It used to belong to Tyra, Terra's child.

"You have a spirit. Who could it be?" Rose asked.

"I don't know. It couldn't be my child. She was taken away, but I never knew what happened to her after that."

The communication continued. "Are you Tyra Green?" Rose asked and the horse rocked in response.

"I tried to find my child but never did. If they never had taken her from me this wouldn't have happened. I don't believe this. Are you my child? Do it again for yes," Terra asked. The rocking horse rocked. "I need to find her death certificate. I need to know what happened and that she can rest in peace. How can we get her to behave? She probably just wanted me to know."

"Play her game. Build her a room up here. Maybe she needs your help," Rose responded. "Now let's get out of here before something bad happens." Terra agreed and they rolled up the velvet covering after blowing out the candle.

"I'm going to the hospital tomorrow then I'll see if I can find a record of death certificates and obituaries. There may be a mystery here," Terra said.

"OK, I'll be here tonight so if you ever need any help just ask me," Rose offered.

"Great thanks." They both headed to their rooms for a while. During the night they heard two loud bangs coming from the attic. It was obviously the child ghost and when walking by the attic they could hear the horse rocking, so Terra shut the door. Both friends locked their bedroom doors and went to sleep.

Rose came to the living room ready to leave with her bag. "Alright, I've got to go visit my husband at the hospital. He's sicker." She felt angry that her husband was still sick and wanted to put an end to the galvanism machine Terra used but didn't know how. Asking her again may not do the trick. It was the thing that brought Terra to life. The morning sky darkened. It looked as if it would rain. A light November rain began to fall, and Rose walked quickly to the hospital.

Rusty's eyes were shut. The heart monitor beeped. He was not responding to antibiotics. "Sleep soundly Rusty," she said into his ear. He opened his eyes for just a few seconds and his monitor flat lined and five medical people came rushing in. Moments later he was pronounced dead. Rose cried hysterically. She missed him immediately. "Goodbye," was all that came from her lips wondering why this happened and what she would do. An immediate depression fell upon her, and she sat next to his body for quite a while.

That afternoon Rose knocked on Terra's door. The mansion looked wonderful. The outside had fresh white paint and the grass watered, and when she opened the door the inside was cozy and spacious, not vintage at all. "I need to know where the jar is buried. I don't want my husband in the same cemetery as a jar with the ghosts who killed him."

"In the one across from the local Baptist church."

"He died this morning."

"I'm sorry. Please come in." Terra shook her head. She had no idea the Frankenstein's would attack

Rusty, but it was foolish to bring them back after they attacked her. It was done to mock them the way they mocked her. They saw how it felt. They kidnapped her like a circus freak. She couldn't even feel their knife wound when they cut her. They might have forgotten she was already dead. Another reason to bring them back was to control them. They could have been her slaves but that never happened.

"He didn't live long after he got sick. I miss him already. His funeral will be this weekend."

"I hope you feel happy again soon. Keep in touch. I will call you if I need you."

"Okay. The place looks good. Do you still have all the galvanism equipment?" Rose could see the place was clean.

"I brought it. It's in the backyard shed. I know I should, but it's hard to give up," Terra said.

"My husband died because of it. Is it really that easy to bring someone back to life?"

"If they've just died it is."

"I'd better be going. I don't think you should bring people to life again."

"I know. Do you want to come over for lunch later?" Terra asked.

"I don't think I'll be up to it. I have a funeral to plan for. Is there any way we can get rid of that machine?"

"Yes, we need to, but I don't know how to disassemble it. It's too big to throw out." Terra lied. She knew she wanted it, and she also knew it was dangerous.

Roses eyes lit up. "You can come to my husband's funeral. I'll be in contact." Quickly Rose was gone.

Terra had wanted to give up the galvanism machine before but didn't think it could be done forever. She covered it with a blanket and forgot about it for a while in the shed. A hard rain began to fall on Terra. It was like punishment. The problem would rest in peace for now.

***

Rose lit another candle on her husband's grave. Six red roses were laid there. It had stopped snowing but was very cold that December.

She spent every weekend for the following four months at his gravestone. She quit her psychic job and laid low for a while. When the flowers came up in March, she spent her time gardening for herself and other people. Every now and then she would tell her own future at home. She and Terra did not talk due to Rusty's death. Rose never forgot it and wondered what Terra was up to. The urge to spy on her was strong. That night she spent the night it seemed Terra was dead and didn't want friends although she was friendly. Terra seemed to be afraid but there's no way she was afraid of the dead, she just didn't want to deal with them.

That March with candles lit she read her crystal ball and saw what made Terra so different. She was dead and looked like a goddess when Rose asked, "Will Terra die again?" It showed Terra in a gray dress, standing in her cemetery with electricity all around her. In front of her lay a single red rose. It turned green and blue lightning flashed in the back of her. She was not only undead, but very strong and one with nature. It was obvious she was dead because she was in a graveyard decomposing but there she stood next to her freshly dug grave that Dr. Frankenstein dug. The gravestone only read Terra Belinda Green. Rose believed one day all the trouble she caused would come back to Terra again, and she didn't really want to be there when it did. Her profession as a psychic ghost hunter was all she needed to equip her for their future meetings. Rose was one of the best.

Did you love *Frankenstein's Bride: A Mystery*? Then you should read *Found In Misty Falls*[1] by Martha Wickham!

[2]

Violet's life is about to change to more powerful. When she is hiking through Misty Falls she stumbles upon a ring. When she tells her parents they find the owner and uncover a story of how it became magical. She uses it to her advantage, but when an accident happens she must rethink keeping it.Her life is turned upside down. The ring can do good and bad. It all must come to an end.Review"Absolutely amazing..highly recommended." -Mai, Goodreads

Read more at https://readmarthawickham.com/.

---

1. https://books2read.com/u/boMadL

2. https://books2read.com/u/boMadL

Also by Martha Wickham

A Cursed Antique
Stories of a Cursed Antique
Found In Misty Falls
Beware of a Cursed Forest

Circle of Roses
Frankenstein's Bride: A Mystery
Circle Of Roses
The Haunted Rosebuds
Emily's Darkness
Tyra of the Shadows
Abigail's Road of Terror
The Rose Cases: Sylvie's Diary
Mystery of Frankenstein's Bride Collection: Ghosts of the Circle

Witch Lane
Nightmare in a Bottle
Midnight at Witch Lane

Herbs and Ashes: Dust of Despair

Standalone
Garden Of Desire
Led By Obsession
Relaxed Poetry
Wishes, Gems, Disasters
Woodland Escape
Flames Of Fate

Watch for more at https://readmarthawickham.com/.

About the Author

Martha has studied writing with Writer's Digest and has an associate's degree. She has also written poems and songs and has even studied screen writing and horror at one time. She still practices writing and likes getting writing prompts, and her favorite author is VC Andrews. Listen to her hot new audiobooks at your favorite retailer.

Read more at https://readmarthawickham.com/.